For Simi
A. McA.

For Vicki,
without whom this would not
have been possible.
C.F.

First published in 2003 in Great Britain by

GULLANE
CHILDREN'S BOOKS

Winchester House, 259-269 Old Marylebone Road,
London NW1 5XJ

Library of Congress-in-Publication Data Available

10 9 8 7 6 5 4 3 2 1

Published in 2003 by Sterling Publishing Co., Inc.
387 Park Avenue South
New York, NY 10016

Distributed in Canada by Sterling Publishing
c/o Canadian Manda Group
One Atlantic Avenue, Suite 105
Toronto, Ontario, Canada M6K 3E7

Text © Angela McAllister 2003
Illustrations © Charles Fuge 2003

Sterling ISBN 1-4027-0708-8

Found You, Little Wombat!

Angela McAllister • Charles Fuge

Sterling Publishing Co., Inc.
New York

Little Wombat was playing
hide-and-seek with Rabbit and Koala.

"Found you!" said Koala.

"Now it's your turn to seek,
Little Wombat!" said Rabbit.

Rabbit and Koala hid,
and so did Little Wombat.

They waited and waited . . .
and tried to keep very quiet.
So did Little Wombat!

"Let's start again!" said Koala with a chuckle. "You have to count to ten and then come and find us." Little Wombat shut his eyes. "Two, TEN!"

"No, no! Count ten flowers before you come and find us," called Rabbit and Koala, as they ran away to hide.

"One . . ." counted Little Wombat.
But he soon became distracted
and began to look around.

Little Wombat wandered over a hill to see what was on the other side . . .

He didn't notice a cloud
creep in front of the sun.
He didn't notice the sky turn gray.
He didn't notice the wind
shake the trees.

He suddenly remembered that Rabbit and Koala were hiding. "Ten! I'm coming!" he shouted.

But where was Koala?
Where was Rabbit?
Little Wombat felt all alone.
"Where am I?" he asked.

DRIP . . . DRIP.
Raindrops started to fall
from a small, dark cloud.

DRIP . . . DRIP.
Teardrops started to fall
from a small, lost wombat.

But the sun didn't hide for long.
And neither did Little Wombat.
"Hmm, that's a very wobbly
toadstool . . .

. . . found you!" said Mom.
"What a clever umbrella!"

"Let's splash in the puddles on the way home," said Rabbit. So Little Wombat jumped and made the biggest, happiest splash of all.